For my love, - PF

For Beth, - MH

First Edition Project Books
Published by Southwest Human Development
2850 North 24th Street, Phoenix, AZ 85008

USA

First Edition 2016
Text Copyright © 2016 by Phoebe Fox
Illustration Copyright © 2016 by Michael Hale

Library of Congress Control Number: 2016908970
Fox, Phoebe, author
Hale, Michael, illustrator
Up Up Up / Fox and Hale
32 p.

Summary: *"Ten animals are invited to a party, but on their
way up to the 10th floor they take a humorous detour"* - Provided by publisher.

Manufactured in China by PRC Book Printing
ISBN 978-0 692-72770-6
10 9 8 7 6 5 4 3 2 1

Design by Michael Hale
Text set in Janda Snickerdoodle Serif Bold

UP UP UP

by Phoebe Fox

illustrated by Michael Hale

Mouse
crawls in

Squeak

Squeak

Squeak

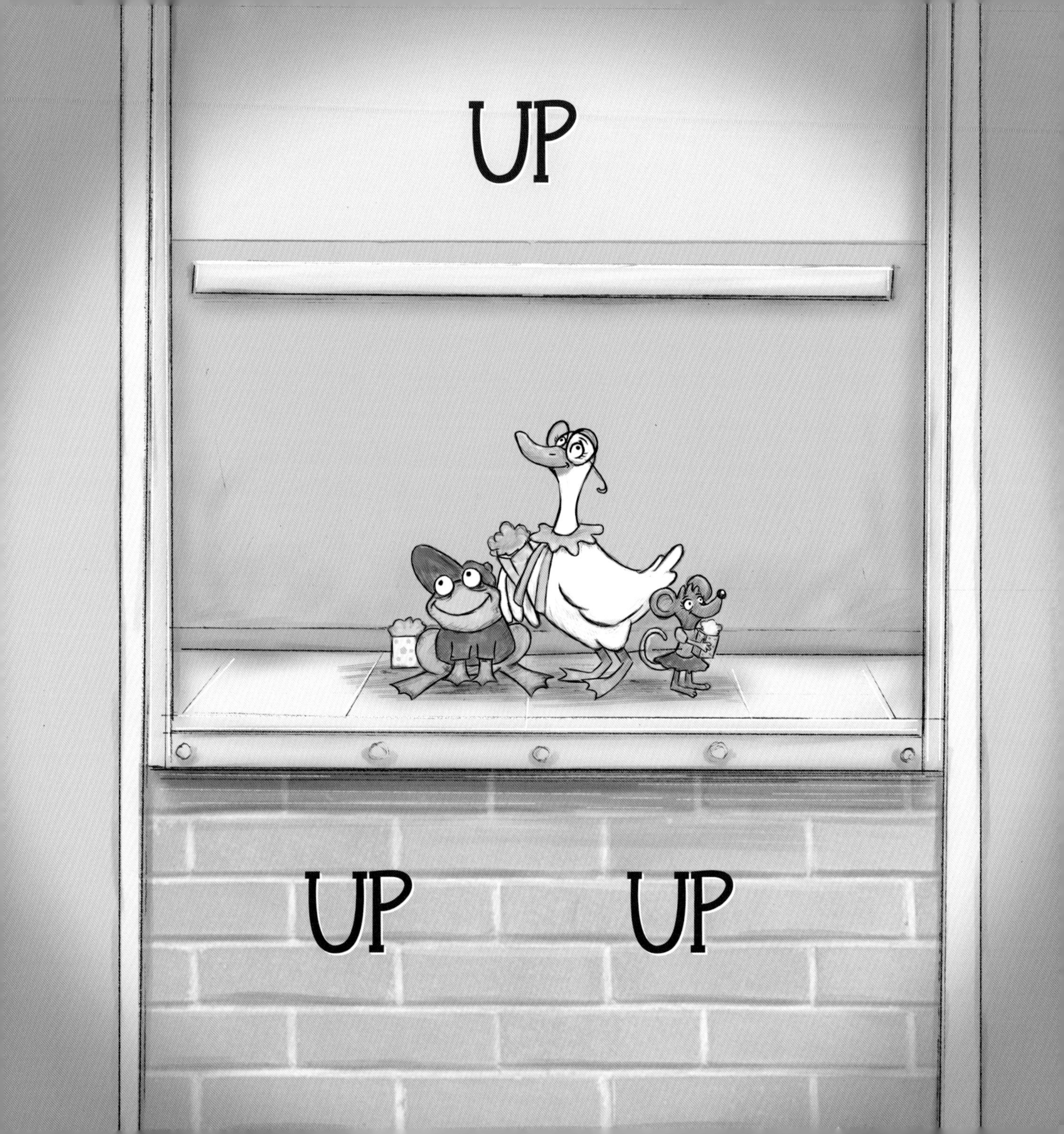

UP

UP UP

UP UP UP

Bear pads in

Grrr Grrr Grrr